Samuel Epes Turner

Life of Charlemagne of Eginhard

Samuel Epes Turner

Life of Charlemagne of Eginhard

ISBN/EAN: 9783742891761

Manufactured in Europe, USA, Canada, Australia, Japa

Cover: Foto ©Raphael Reischuk / pixelio.de

Manufactured and distributed by brebook publishing software
(www.brebook.com)

Samuel Epes Turner

Life of Charlemagne of Eginhard

CONTENTS.

LIFE OF EGINHARD.

EGINHARD, called also Einhard, was born in
770 in the Maingau, a canton in the country of
the Eastern Franks lying along the river Main.
His parents, Eginhard (Einhard) and Engelfrit,
sent him to the Monastery of Fulda to be edu-
cated, and in course of time the abbot, Baugolf,
presented him at court. Charlemagne recognized his talents and made him minister of public works and councillor, besides employing him
as his private secretary. Lewis the Pious retained him in all these offices, and showered favours upon him. In 815 he gave him the estates
of Michlinstat and Mulinheim, and the same year
appointed him abbot of Blandinium, near Ghent;
about 816 he made him abbot of Fontenelle, near
Rouen, and in 819 abbot of St. Bavo, in Ghent.
It appears from certain of Eginhard's writings
that he also held the abbacy of St. Servatius, in
Maestricht, the abbacy of St. Chlodowald (the
site of this monastery is unknown), the Church
of St. John the Baptist, in Pavia, and a fief at
Frideslare, in Hesse.

He was sent by Charlemagne to Rome in 806,
to obtain the confirmation of his will from Leo
III.

Eginhard is supposed to have entered the

ranks of the Church in 815, but he did not retire from active life until 830.   He then betook himself to the Benedictine monastery of Seligenstadt, in Mulinheim, founded by him three years previously in honour of St. Marcellinus and St. Peter, whose relics he had been at great pains to bring from Rome and enshrine.

Nothing is known of Eginhard's personal appearance, except that he was a small man.   He was married, and his wife's name was Emma, but her origin is wrapt in obscurity. So far as known, their marriage was not blessed with children.

The famous legend of Eginhard and Emma, in which she figures as Charlemagne's daughter, is wholly mythical; it was first committed to writing in 1180, by a monk of the monastery of Lorsch, which Eginhard had endowed.   William of Malmesbury, whose chronicle ends with the year 1142, tells a similar story of the sister of the Emperor Henry III.

Emma died in 836.   Eginhard died a few years later, in the Abbey of Seligenstadt; the date of his death is variously given.

It is by no means certain that Eginhard wrote the "Annals" attributed to him; but the "Life of Charlemagne," his "Letters," and his "Account of the Transfer of the Relics of St. Marcellinus and St. Peter" are of undoubted authenticity.   No other works of his have come down to us.   The style of the "Life of Charlemagne" is a palpable imitation of Suetonius.

PREFACE.

SINCE I have taken upon myself to narrate the public and private life, and no small part of the deeds, of my lord and foster-father, the most excellent and most justly renowned King Charles, I have condensed the matter into as brief a form as possible. I have been careful not to omit any facts that could come to my knowledge, but at the same time not to offend by a prolix style those minds that despise everything modern, if one can possibly avoid offending by a new work men who seem to despise also the masterpieces of antiquity, the works of most learned and luminous writers. Very many of them, I have no doubt, are men devoted to a life of literary leisure, who feel that the affairs of the present generation ought not to be passed by,

and who do not consider everything done
to-day as unworthy of mention and deserving to be given over to silence and oblivion,
but are nevertheless seduced by lust of im-
mortality to celebrate the glorious deeds
of other times by some sort of composition
rather than to deprive posterity of the mention of their own names by not writing at all.

Be this as it may, I see no reason why I
should refrain from entering upon a task of
this kind, since no man can write with more
accuracv than 1 of events that took place
about me, and of facts concerning which I
had personal knowledge, ocular demonstra-
tion, as the saying goes, and I have no
means of ascertaining whether or not any
one else has the subject in hand.

In any event, I would rather commit my
story to writing, and hand it down to posterity in partnership with others, so to
speak, than to suffer the most glorious life
of this most excellent king, the greatest of
all the princes of his day, and his illustrious deeds, hard for men of later times to

imitate, to be wrapt in the darkness of oblivion.

But there are still other reasons, neither unwarrantable nor insufficient, in my opinion, that urge me to write on this subject, namely, the care that King Charles bestowed upon me in my childhood, and my constant friendship with himself and his children after I began to take up my abode at court. In this way he strongly endeared me to himself, and made me greatly his debtor as well in death as in life; so that were I, unmindful of the benefits conferred upon me, to keep silence concerning the most glorious and illustrious deeds of a man who claims so much at my hands, and suffer his life to lack due eulogy and written memorial, as if he had never lived, I should deservedly appear ungrateful, and be so considered, albeit my powers are feeble, scanty, next to nothing indeed, and not at all adapted to write and set forth a life that would tax the eloquence of a Tully.

I submit the book. It contains the his-

tory of a very great and distinguished man;
but there is nothing in it to wonder at besides his deeds, except the fact that I, who
am a barbarian, and very little versed in
the Roman language, seem to suppose myself capable of writing gracefully and re-
spectably in Latin, and to carry my pre-
sumption so far as to disdain the sentiment
that Cicero is said in the first book of the
"Tusculan Disputations" to have expressed when speaking of the Latin authors.
His words are: " It is an outrageous abuse
both of time and literature for a man to
commit his thoughts to writing without
having the ability either to arrange them
or elucidate them, or attract readers by
some charm of style." This dictum of the
famous orator might have deterred me from
writing if I had not made up my mind that
it was better to risk the opinions of the
world, and put my little talents for composition to the test, than to slight the memory
of so great a man for the sake of sparing
myself.

LIFE

OF THE

EMPEROR CHARLES.

---

1. THE Merovingian family, from which the Franks used to choose their kings, is commonly said to have lasted until the time of Childeric,[1] who was deposed, shaved, and thrust into the cloister by command of the Roman Pontiff Stephen.[2] But although, to all outward appearance, it ended with him, it had long since been devoid of vital strength, and conspicuous only from bearing the empty

751-752.

---

[1] Childeric III., 743-752.

[2] Stephen II. (or III.), 752-757. He anointed Pepin in 754. His predecessor, Zacharias, had ordered the deposition of Childeric just before his death, in 752.

epithet Royal; the real power and authority in the kingdom lay in the hands of the
chief officer of the court, the so-called Mayor
of the Palace, and he was at the head of
affairs. There was nothing left the King
to do but to be content with his name of
King, his flowing hair, and long beard;[3] to
sit on his throne and play the ruler; to give
ear to the ambassadors that came from all
quarters, and to dismiss them, as if on his
own responsibility, in words that were, in
fact, suggested to him, or even imposed
upon him. He had nothing that he could
call his own beyond this vain title of King,
and the precarious support allowed by the
Mayor of the Palace in his discretion, except a single country-seat, that brought
him but a very small income. There was a
dwelling-house upon this, and a small number of servants attached to it, sufficient to
perform the necessary offices. When he had

---

[3] The badge of honour and freedom. See
Grimm's "Deutsche Rechtsalterthümer," pp.
146, 239.

to go abroad, he used to ride in a cart, drawn by a yoke of oxen,[*] driven, peasant-fashion, by a ploughman; he rode in this way to the palace and to the general assembly of the people, that met once a year for the welfare of the kingdom, and he returned home in like manner. The Mayor of the Palace took charge of the government, and of everything that had to be planned or executed at home or abroad.

II. At the time of Childeric's deposition, Pepin, the father of King Charles, held this office of Mayor of the Palace, one might almost say, by hereditary right; for Pepin's father, Charles, had received it at the hands of his father, Pepin, and filled it with distinction. It was this Charles that crushed the tyrants who claimed to rule the whole Frank land as their own, and that utterly routed the Saracens, when they attempted the conquest of Gaul, in two

715–741

---

[*] An ancient royal custom, according to Grimm's "Deutsche Rechtsalterthümer," p. 262.

2

great battles—one in Aquitania, near the
town of Poitiers, and the other on the River Berre,[s] near Narbonne—and compelled
them to return to Spain. This honour was
usually conferred by the people only upon
men eminent from their illustrious birth
and ample wealth. For some years, osten-
sibly under King Childeric, Pepin, the father of King Charles, shared the
741. duties inherited from his father
and grandfather most amicably with his
brother, Carloman. The latter, then, for
reasons unknown, renounced the heavy
cares of an earthly crown and re-
747. tired to Rome. Here he exchanged
his worldly garb for a cowl, and built a
monastery on Mt. Oreste, near the Church
of St. Sylvester, where he enjoyed for several years the seclusion that he desired, in
company with certain others who had the
same object in view. But so many distinguished Franks made the pilgrimage to

---

[s] Not L'Étang de Berre, but a small stream
emptying into L'Étang de Sijean.

Rome to fulfil their vows, and insisted upon paying their respects to him, as their former lord, on the way, that the repose which he so much loved was broken by these frequent visits, and he was driven to change his abode. Accordingly, when he found that his plans were frustrated by his many visitors, he abandoned the mountain, and withdrew to the Monastery of St. Benedict, on Monte Casino, in the province of Samnium, and passed the rest of his days there in the exercises of religion.

754.

III. Pepin, however, was raised, by decree of the Roman Pontiff, from the rank of Mayor of the Palace to that of King, and ruled alone over the Franks for fifteen years or more.[6] He died of dropsy, in Paris, at the close of the Aquitanian war,[7] which he had waged with William, Duke of Aquitania, for nine successive

752-768.

768.
Sept. 24.

760-768.

---

[6] In fact more than sixteen years.
[7] See V., p. 22.

years, and left two sons, Charles and Carloman, upon whom, by the grace of God, the
succession devolved.

    The Franks, in a general assembly of the
768.   people, made them both kings, on
Oct. 9.   condition that they should di-
vide the whole kingdom equally between
them, Charles to take and rule the part that
had belonged to their father, Pepin, and
Carloman the part which their uncle, Carloman, had governed.* The conditions
were accepted, and each entered into possession of the share of the kingdom that .
fell to him by this arrangement; but peace
was only maintained between them with
the greatest difficulty, because many of
Carloman's party kept trying to disturb
their good understanding, and there were
some even who plotted to involve them in
a war with each other. The event, however, showed the danger to have been rather imaginary than real, for at Carloman's

---

* This account of the division is somewhat
inaccurate.

death his widow[9] fled to Italy with her
sons[10] and her principal adher-   771.
ents, and without reason, despite   Dec. 4.
her husband's brother, put herself and her
children under the protection of Desiderius, King of the Lombards. Carloman had
succumbed to disease after ruling two
years[11] in common with his brother, and at
his death Charles was unanimously elected
King of the Franks.

IV. It would be folly, I think, to write a
word concerning Charles's birth[12] and infancy, or even his boyhood, for nothing has ever
been written on the subject, and there is no
one alive now who can give information of
it. Accordingly, I have determined to pass

---

[9] Gerberga.

[10] One was named Pepin.

[11] In fact more than three years.

[12] Charles was born in 742. See XXX. and
XXXI. The day of his birth is supposed to
have been April 2d, on the testimony of a ninth-
century calendar of the Monastery of Lorsch.
The place of his birth is wholly uncertain. See
Mabillon's "De Re Diplomaticâ Suppl." cap. IX.

that by as unknown, and to proceed at onc.
to treat of his character, his deeds, and such
other facts of his life as are worth telling and
setting forth, and shall first give an account
of his deeds at home and abroad, then of his
character and pursuits, and lastly of his ad-
ministration and death, omitting nothing
worth knowing or necessary to know.

V. His first undertaking in a military
way was the Aquitanian war,[12] be-
769.   gun by his father, but not brought
to a close; and because he thought that it
could be readily carried through, he took it
up while his brother was yet alive, calling
upon him to render aid. The campaign once
opened, he conducted it with the greatest
vigour, notwithstanding his brother with-
held the assistance that he had promised,
and did not desist or shrink from his self-
imposed task until, by his patience and firm-
ness, he had completely gained his ends.
He compelled Hunold, who had attempt-

----

[12] See III., p. 19.

ed to seize Aquitania after Waifar's death, and renew the war then almost concluded, to abandon Aquitania and flee to Gascony. Even here he gave him no rest, but crossed the River Garonne, built the Castle of Fronsac, and sent ambassadors to Lupus, Duke of Gascony, to demand the surrender of the fugitive, threatening to take him by force unless he were promptly given up to him. Thereupon Lupus chose the wiser course, and not only gave Hunold up, but submitted himself, with the province which he ruled, to the King.

VI. After bringing this war to an end and settling matters in Aquitania (his associate in authority had meantime departed this life), he was induced, by the prayers and entreaties of Hadrian,[14] Bishop of the city of Rome, to wage war on the Lombards. His father before him had undertaken this task at the request of Pope Stephen,[15] but under great

773.

---

[14] Hadrian I., 772-795.
[15] Stephen II. (or III.), 752-757.

difficulties; for certain leading Franks, of
whom he usually took counsel, had so ve-
hemently opposed his design as to declare
openly that they would leave the King and
go home.   Nevertheless, the war against
the Lombard king, Astolf, had
754.
been taken up and very quickly
concluded.   Now, although Charles seems
to have had similar, or rather just the same
grounds for declaring war that his father
had, the war itself differed from the preceding one alike in its difficulties and its
issue.   Pepin, to be sure, after besieging
King Astolf a few days in Pavia, had compelled him to give hostages, to restore to the
Romans the cities and castles that he had
taken, and to make oath that he would not
attempt to seize them again : but Charles
did not cease, after declaring war,
773.
until he had exhausted King Desiderius by a long siege, and forced him
to surrender at discretion; driven
774.
his son Adalgis, the last hope of
the Lombards. not only from his kingdom,

but from all Italy; restored to the Romans all that they had lost; subdued Hruodgaus, Duke of Friuli, who was plotting revolution; reduced all Italy to his power, and set his son Pepin as king over it. 776. 781.

At this point I should describe Charles's difficult passage over the Alps into Italy, and the hardships that the Franks endured in climbing the trackless mountain-ridges, the heaven-aspiring cliffs and ragged peaks, if it were not my purpose iu this work to record the manner of his life rather than the incidents of the wars that he waged. Suffice it to say that this war ended with the subjection of Italy, the banishment of King Desiderius for life, the expulsion of his son Adalgis from Italy, and the restoration of the conquests of the Lombard kings to Hadrian, the head of the Roman Church.

VII. At the conclusion of this struggle, the Saxon war, that seems to have been only laid aside for the time, was taken up again.

B

No war ever undertaken by the Frank nation was carried on with such persistence
and bitterness, or cost so much labour, because the Saxons, like almost all the tribes
of Germany, were a fierce people, given to
the worship of devils, and hostile to our religion, and did not consider it dishonoura-
ble to transgress and violate all law, human
and divine.   Then there were peculiar cir-
cumstances that tended to cause a breach of
peace every day.   Except in a few places,
where large forests or mountain-ridges in-
tervened and made the bounds certain,
the line between ourselves and the Saxons
passed almost in its whole extent through
an open country, so that there was no end
to the murders, thefts, and arsons on both
sides.   In this way the Franks became so
embittered that they at last re-
772   solved to make reprisals no longer, but to come to open war with the Saxons.
Accordingly war was begun against
772-804.   them, and was waged for thirty-
three successive years with great fury ;

more, however, to the disadvantage of the
Saxons than of the Franks. It could
doubtless have been brought to an end
sooner, had it not been for the faithlessness
of the Saxons. It is hard to say how often
they were conquered, and, humbly submit-
ting to the King, promised to do what was en-
joined upon them, gave without hesitation
the required hostages, and received the officers sent them from the King. They were
sometimes so much weakened and reduced
that they promised to renounce the worship of devils, and to adopt Christianity;
but they were no less ready to violate these
terms than prompt to accept them, so that
it is impossible to tell which came easier to
them to do; scarcely a year passed from
the beginning of the war without such
changes on their part. But the King did
not suffer his high purpose and steadfast-
ness—firm alike in good and evil fortune—
to be wearied by any fickleness on their
part, or to be turned from the task that he
had undertaken; on the contrary, he never

allowed their faithless behaviour to go un-
punished, but either took the field against
them in person, or sent his counts with an
army to wreak vengeance[16] and exact right-
eous satisfaction. At last, after conquering
and subduing all who had offered resist-

804.   ance, he took ten thousand of
those that lived on the banks of
the Elbe, and settled them, with their wives
and children, in many different bodies here
and there in Gaul and Germany. The war
that had lasted so many years was at length
ended by their acceding to the terms offered by the King; which were renunciation
of their national religious customs and the
worship of devils, acceptance of the sacra-
ments of the Christian faith and religion, and
union with the Franks to form one people.

VIII. Charles himself fought but two

788.   pitched battles in this war, although it was long protracted—

---

[16] At the time of Witikind's great revolt in
782, Charles had 4500 Saxons beheaded in one
day at Verden, on the Aller.

one on Mount Osning,[17] at the place called Detmold, and again on the bank of the river Hase,[18] both in the space of little more than a month. The enemy were so routed and overthrown in these two battles that they never afterwards ventured to take the offensive or to resist the attacks of the King, unless they were protected by a strong position. A great many of the Frank as well as of the Saxon nobility, men occupying the highest posts of honour, perished in this war, which only came to an end after the lapse of thirty-two years. 804.

So many and grievous were the wars that were declared against the Franks in the meantime, and skilfully conducted by the King, that one may reasonably question whether his fortitude or his good fortune is to be more admired. The Saxon war

---

[17] The Lippescher Wald, a part of the great Teutoburger Wald.

[18] Near Osnabrück, at a place called, in the Middle Ages, Schlachtvörderberg, now known as Die Clûs.

began two years before the Italian war;[19] ·
but although it went on without interrup-
tion, business elsewhere was not neglected,
nor was there any shrinking from other
equally arduous contests. The King, who
excelled all the princes of his time in wis-
dom and greatness of soul, did not suffer
difficulty to deter him or danger to daunt
him from anything that had to be taken
up or carried through, for he had trained
himself to bear and endure whatever came,
without yielding in adversity, or trusting
to the deceitful favours of fortune in pros-
perity.

IX. In the midst of this vigorous and
almost uninterrupted struggle with the Saxons, he covered the frontier by garrisons at

778.   the proper points, and marched
          over the Pyrenees into Spain at
the head of all the forces that he could
muster. All the towns and castles that he
attacked surrendered, and up to the time

[19] The Saxon war began in 772; the Italian war
in 773

of his homeward march he sustained no loss whatever; but on his return through the Pyrenees he had cause to rue the treachery of the Gascons. That region is well adapted for ambuscades by reason of the thick forests that cover it; and as the army was advancing in the long line of march necessitated by the narrowness of the road, the Gascons, who lay in ambush on the top of a very high mountain, attacked the rear of the baggage-train and the rear-guard in charge of it, and hurled them down to the very bottom of the valley.[30] In the struggle that ensued, they cut them off to a man; they then plundered the baggage, and dispersed with all speed in every direction under cover of approaching night. The lightness of their armour and the nature of the battle-ground stood the Gascons in good stead on this occasion, whereas the Franks fought at a disadvantage in every respect, because of the

778.

---

[30] Roncesvalles.

weight of their armour and the unevenness
of the ground.   Eggihard, the King's stew-
ard ; Anselm, Count Palatine ; and Roland,[21]
Governor of the March of Brittany, with very
many others, fell in this engagement.   This
ill turn could not be avenged for the nonce,
because the enemy scattered so widely after
carrying out their plan that not the least
? clew could be had to their whereabouts.

    X. Charles also subdued the Bretons, who
live on the sea-coast, in the ex-
786.   treme western part of Gaul. When
they refused to obey him, he sent an army
against them, and compelled them to give
hostages, and to promise to do his bidding.

    He afterwards entered Italy in per-
son with his army, and passed
787.
through Rome to Capua, a city in Cam-
pania, where he pitched his camp and
threatened the Beneventans with hostilities
unless they should submit themselves to
him.   Their duke, Aragis, escaped the dan-

---

   [21] This is the only mention in *history* of this
famous character.

ger by sending his two sons, Rumold and Grimold, with a great sum of money to meet the King, begging him to accept them as hostages, and promising for himself and his people compliance with all the King's commands, on the single condition that his personal attendance should not be required. The King took the welfare of the people into account rather than the stubborn disposition of the Duke, accepted the proffered hostages, and released him from the obligation to appear before him in consideration of his handsome gift. He retained the younger son only as hostage, and sent the elder back to his father, and returned to Rome, leaving commissioners with Aragis to exact the oath of allegiance, and administer it to the Beneventans. He stayed in Rome several days in order to pay his devotions at the holy places, and then came back to Gaul.   787.

XI. At this time, on a sudden, the Bavarian war broke out, but came to a speedy end. It was due to the arrogance and folly

8

of Duke Tassilo. His wife,[22] a daughter
of King Desiderius, was desirous of aveng-
ing her father's banishment through the
agency of her husband, and accordingly induced him to make a treaty with the Huns,
the neighbours of the Bavarians on the east,
and not only to leave the King's commands
unfulfilled, but to challenge him to war.
Charles's high spirit could not brook Tassilo's insubordination, for it seemed to him
to pass all bounds; accordingly he straight-
way summoned his troops from all sides for
a campaign against Bavaria, and appeared
in person with a great army on the river
Lech, which forms the boundary between
the Bavarians and the Alemanni. After
pitching his camp upon its banks, he determined to put the Duke's disposition to the
test by an embassy before entering the province. Tassilo did not think that it was for
his own or his people's good to persist, so
he surrendered himself to the King, gave

---

[22] Liutberga.

the hostages demanded, among them his own son Theodo, and promised by oath not to give ear to any one who should attempt to turn him from his allegiance; so this war, which bade fair to be very grievous, came very quickly to an end. Tassilo, however, was afterwards summoned to the King's presence, and not suffered to depart, and the government of the province that he had had in charge was no longer intrusted to a duke, but to counts.

788.

XII. After these uprisings had been thus quelled, war was declared against the Slaves who are commonly known among us as Wilzi, but properly, that is to say in their own tongue, are called Welatabians. The Saxons served in this campaign as auxiliaries among the tribes that followed the King's standard at his summons, but their obedience lacked sincerity and devotion. War was declared because the Slaves kept harassing the Abodriti, old allies of the Franks, by continual raids, in spite of all commands to the con-

789.

trary. A gulf[23] of unknown length, but nowhere more than a hundred miles wide,
and in many parts narrower, stretches off
towards the east from the Western Ocean.
Many tribes have settlements on its shores;
the Danes and Swedes, whom we call Northmen, on the northern shore and all the ad-
jacent islands; but the southern shore is inhabited by the Slaves and Aïsti,[24] and vari-
ous other tribes. The Welatabians, against
whom the King now made war, were the
chief of these; but in a single campaign,
which he conducted in person, he
so crushed and subdued them that
they did not think it advisable thereafter
to refuse obedience to his commands.

789.

XIII. The war against the Avars, or
Huns,[25] followed, and, except the
Saxon war, was the greatest that
he waged; he took it up with more spirit

791.

---

[23] The Baltic Sea.

[24] Modern Esthonia owes its name to the Aïsti.

[25] The Huns had aided and abetted Tassilo.
See XI. p. 34.

than any of his other wars, and made far
greater preparations for it. He
conducted one campaign in per-   791.
son in Pannonia, of which the Huns then
had possession. He intrusted all subse-
quent operations to his son, Pepin, and the
governors of the provinces, to counts even,
and lieutenants. Although they most vig-
orously prosecuted the war, it only came to
a conclusion after a seven years' struggle.
The utter depopulation of Pannonia, and
the site of the Khan's palace, now a desert,
where not a trace of human habitation is
visible, bear witness how many battles were
fought in those years, and how much blood
was shed. The entire body of the Hun
nobility perished in this contest, and all its
glory with it. All the money and treasure
that had been years amassing was seized,
and no war in which the Franks have ever
engaged within the memory of man brought
them such riches and such booty. Up to
that time the Huns had passed²⁶ for a poor

²⁶ The subject of the verb is not expressed in

people, but so much gold and silver was found in the Khan's palace, and so much valuable spoil taken in battle, that one may well think that the Franks took justly from the Huns what the Huns had formerly taken unjustly from other nations. Only two of the chief men of the Franks fell in this war

799. —Eric, Duke of Friuli, who was killed in Tarsatch,[37] a town on the coast of Liburnia, by the treachery of the inhabitants; and Gerold,[38] Governor of Ba-

799. varia, who met his death in Pau- nonia, slain, with two men that were accompanying him, by an unknown hand while he was marshalling his forces for battle against the Huns, and riding up and down the line encouraging his men.

---

the original, and this passage is commonly rendered "The Franks had passed," etc., which makes the sentence meaningless.

[37] The Tarsatica of olden time, very near Tarsaticum (Fiume).

[38] He was brother to Hildegard, Charles's wife.

This war was otherwise almost a bloodless one so far as the Franks were concerned, and ended most satisfactorily, although by reason of its magnitude it was long protracted.

XIV. The Saxon war next came to an end as successful as the struggle had been long. The Bohemian and Linonian wars[39] that next broke out could not last long; 805-808. both were quickly carried through under the leadership of the younger Charles. The last of these wars was the one declared against the Northmen called Danes. They began their career as pirates, but afterwards took to laying waste the coasts of Gaul and Germany with their large fleet. Their King, Godfred, was so puffed with vain aspirations that he counted on gaining empire over all Germany, and looked upon Saxony and Frisia as his provinces. He had already subdued his neighbours the Abo-

[39] Bohemian war, 805-806; Linonian war, 808.

driti, and made them tributary, and boast-
ed that he would shortly appear with a
great army before Aix-la-Chapelle, where
the King held his court. Some faith was
put in his words, empty as they sound, and
it is supposed that he would have attempted something of the sort if he had not
been prevented by a premature death. He
was murdered by one of his own
810. body-guard, and so ended at once
his life and the war that he had begun.

XV. Such are the wars, most skilfully
planned and successfully fought, which this
most powerful king waged during the forty-
seven years of his reign.[30] He so largely
increased the Frank kingdom, which was
already great and strong when he received it
at his father's hands, that more than double
its former territory was added to it. The

---

[30] From 9th October, 768, to 28th January, 814,
the date of Charles's death, is little more than
forty-five years. The number forty-seven is ar-
rived at by considering the years 768 and 814 as
complete.

authority of the Franks was formerly confined to that part of Gaul included between the Rhine and the Loire, the Ocean and the Balearic Sea; to that part of Germany which is inhabited by the so-called Eastern Franks, and is bounded by Saxony and the Danube, the Rhine and the Saale—this stream separates the Thuringians from the Sorabians; and to the country of the Alemanni and Bavarians. By the wars above mentioned he first made tributary Aquitania, Gascony, and the whole of the region of the Pyrenees as far as the River Ebro, which rises in the land of the Navarrese, flows through the most fertile districts of Spain, and empties into the Balearic Sea, beneath the walls of the city of Tortosa. He next reduced and made tributary all Italy from Aosta to Lower Calabria, where the boundary-line runs between the Beneventans and the Greeks, a territory more than a thousand miles[31] long; then Sax-

---

[31] Roman miles.

ony, which constitutes no small part of Germany, and is reckoned to be twice as wide as the country inhabited by the Franks, while about equal to it in length; in addition, both Pannonias, Dacia beyond the Danube, and Istria, Liburnia, and Dalmatia, except the cities on the coast, which he left to the Greek Emperor for friendship's sake, and because of the treaty that he had made with him. In fine, he vanquished and made tributary all the wild and barbarous tribes dwelling in Germany between the Rhine and the Vistula, the Ocean and the Danube, all of which speak very much the same language, but differ widely from one another in customs and dress. The chief among them are the Welatabians, the Sorabians, the Abodriti, and the Bohemians, and he had to make war upon these; but the rest, by far the larger number, submitted to him of their own accord.

XVI. He added to the glory of his reign by gaining the good-will of several kings and nations; so close, indeed, was

the alliance that he contracted with Alphonso,[32] King of Galicia and Asturias,
that the latter, when sending letters or ambassadors to Charles, invariably styled himself his man. His munificence won the
kings of the Scots also to pay such defer-
ence to his wishes that they never gave him
any other title than lord, or themselves than
subjects and slaves: there are letters from
them extant[33] in which these feelings in his
regard are expressed. His relations with
Aaron,[34] King of the Persians, who ruled
over almost the whole of the East, India
excepted, were so friendly that this prince
preferred his favour to that of all the kings
and potentates of the earth, and considered
that to him alone marks of honour and
munificence were due. Accordingly, when
the ambassadors sent by Charles to visit
the most holy sepulchre and place of resur-

---

[32] Alphonso II., the Chaste, 791-842.

[33] None of them have come down to us.

[34] The famous Haroun al Raschid, fifth of the
Abassides, 786-809.

rection of our Lord and Saviour presented
themselves before him with gifts, and made
known their master's wishes, he not only
granted what was asked, but gave possession of that holy and blessed spot. When
they returned, he despatched his ambassadors with them, and sent magnificent gifts,
besides stuffs, perfumes, and other rich prod-
ucts of the Eastern lands. A few years before this, Charles had asked him for an ele-
phant, and he sent the only one that he had.
The Emperors of Constantinople, Nicephorus,[35] Michael,[36] and Leo,[37] made advances
to Charles, and sought friendship and alliance with him by several embassies; and
even when the Greeks suspected him of de-
signing to wrest the empire from them, because of his assumption of the title of Emperor, they made a close alliance with him,
that he might have no cause of offence.

---

[35] Nicephorus I., 802–811.
[36] Michael I., 811–813.
[37] Leo V., 813–820.

In fact, the power of the Franks was always viewed by the Greeks and Romans with a jealous eye, whence the Greek proverb "Have the Frank for your friend, but not for your neighbour."

XVII. This King, who showed himself so great in extending his empire and subduing foreign nations, and was constantly occupied with plans to that end, undertook also very many works calculated to adorn and benefit his kipgdom, and brought several of them to completion. Among these, the most deserving of mention are the basilica of the Holy Mother of God at Aix-la-Chapelle, built in the most admirable manner, and a bridge over the Rhine at Mayence, half a mile long, the breadth of the river at this point. This bridge was destroyed by fire the year before Charles died, but, owing to his death so soon after, could not be repaired, although he had intended to rebuild it in stone. He began two palaces[38] of beautiful workman-

813. May.

---

[38] These palaces were both rebuilt by Fred-

ship—one near his manor called Ingelheim,
not far from Mayence; the other at Nime-
guen, on the Waal, the stream that washes
the south side of the island of the Bata-
vians. But, above all, sacred edifices were
the object of his care throughout his whole
kingdom; and whenever he found them
falling to ruin from age, he commanded the
priests and fathers who had charge of them
to repair them, and made sure by commissioners that his instructions were obeyed.
He also fitted out a fleet for the war with
the Northmen; the vessels required for this
purpose were built on the rivers that flow
from Gaul and Germany into the Northern
Ocean. Moreover, since the Northmen con-
tinually overran and laid waste the Gallic
and German coasts, he caused watch and
ward to be kept in all the harbours, and at
the mouths of rivers large enough to admit
the entrance of vessels, to prevent the ene-

erick Barbarossa. The one at Ingelheim is de-
scribed at length by Ermoldus Nigellus, Carm.
iv., 181-282.

my from disembarking; and in the South,
in Narbonensis and Septimania, and along
the whole coast of Italy as far as Rome, he
took the same precautions against the Moors,
who had recently begun their piratical
practices. Hence, Italy suffered no great
harm in his time at the hands of the Moors,
nor Gaul and Germany from the Northmen,
save that the Moors got possession of the
Etruscan town of Civita Vecchia by treachery, and sacked it, and the Northmen har-
ried some of the islands in Frisia off the
German coast.

XVIII. Thus did Charles defend and increase as well as beautify his kingdom, as
is well known; and here let me express my
admiration of his great qualities and his
extraordinary constancy alike in good and
evil fortune. I will now forthwith proceed
to give the details of his private and family
life.

After his father's death, while sharing
the kingdom with his brother, he
bore his unfriendliness and jeal-   768–771.

ousy most patiently, and, to the wonder of
all, could not be provoked to be angry with
him.   Later he married a daugh-
770.
ter[39] of Desiderius, King of the
Lombards, at the instance of his mother;
but he repudiated her at the end of a year
for some reason unknown, and married Hildegard, a woman of high birth, of
771.
Suabian origin. He had three sons   3
by her—Charles, Pepin,[40] and Lewis[41]—and
as many daughters[42]—Hruodrud,[43] Bertha,[44]
and Gisela.   He had three other daughters   3

---

[39] Her name is variously given ; perhaps Desi-
derata has the best authority. According to
the Monk of St. Gall, Charles repudiated her because she was an invalid, and unable to bear
children.

[40] He was at first called Carloman, but took
the name of Pepin when he was baptized and
anointed King of Italy by Hadrian I., in 781.

[41] He was one of twins. His twin-brother,
Lothar, died in infancy. See Genealogical Table.

[42] Eginhard omits Adelaide and Hildegard.
See Genealogical Table.

[43] See Note 54.

[44] See Note 98.

·besides these—Theoderada,[45] Hiltrud,[46] and Ruodhaid — two by his third wife, Fastrada, a woman of East Frankish[47] (that is to say, of German) origin, and the third by a concubine, whose name for the moment escapes me.[48] At the death of Fastrada, he married Liutgard, an 794. Alemannic woman, who bore him no children. After her death he had 800 three concubines[49]—Gersuinda, a June 4. Saxon, by whom he had Adaltrud ; Regina,

[45] She became Abbess of Notre Dame d'Argenteuil, near Paris.

[46] She became Abbess of Faremoutiers, according to Father Anselm.

[47] She was the daughter of Rodolph, Count of Franconia.

[48] Supposed by some to have been Himiltrud, mother of Pepin the Hunchback. See Note 58.

[49] Some texts read "four concubines—Mathalgard, who bore him a daughter named Rothild Gersuinda," etc. Those who accept this reading identify Rothild with Rothild, Abbess of Faremoutiers. See the charter published by Mabillon in "Annal. Ord. Bened." ii. p. 745, in which the Emperor Lothar styles the latter "our beloved aunt."

C*   4

who was the mother of Drogo and Hugh;[50] and Ethelind, by whom he had Theodoric.[51] Charles's mother, Berthrada, passed her old age with him in great honour; he entertained the greatest veneration for her; and there was never any disagreement between them except when he divorced the daughter of King Desiderius, whom he had married to please her. She died soon after Hildegard, after living to see three grandsons and as many granddaughters in her son's house, and he buried her with great pomp in the Basilica of St. Denis, where his father lay. He had an only sister,[52] Gisela, who had consecrated herself to a religious life from girlhood, and he

783.

---

[50] They both received the tonsure in 818. Drogo became Bishop of Metz, and died 8th December, 855. Hugh became Abbot of St. Quentin, and died 14th June, 844.

[51] Theodoric, born 810, received the tonsure at the same time with Drogo and Hugh.

[52] Charles had three sisters (see Genealogical Table), but Gisela was for many years the only one surviving.

cherished as much affection for her as for his mother. She also died a few years before him in the nunnery where she had passed her life.[43]

810.

XIX. The plan that he adopted for his children's education was, first of all, to have both boys and girls instructed in the liberal arts, to which he also turned his own attention. As soon as their years admitted, in accordance with the custom of the Franks, the boys had to learn horsemanship, and to practise war and the chase, and the girls to familiarize themselves with cloth-making, and to handle distaff and spindle, that they might not grow indolent through idleness, and he fostered in them every virtuous sentiment. He only lost three of all his children before his death, two sons and one daughter, Charles, who was the eldest, Pepin, whom he had made King of Italy, and Hruodrud, his oldest daughter, whom he had betrothed to Constantine,[44] Emper-

---

[43] At Chelles, near Paris.
[44] Constantine VI., 780–802. Marriage did not

or of the Greeks. Pepin left one son, named Bernard,[55] and five daughters, Adelaide, Atula, Guntrada, Berthaid, and Theoderada. The King gave a striking proof of his

810

fatherly affection at the time of Pepin's death: he appointed the grandson to succeed Pepin, and

813.

had the granddaughters brought up with his own daughters. When his sons and his daughter died, he was not so calm as might have been expected from his remarkably strong mind, for his affections were no less strong, and moved him to

796.

tears. Again, when he was told of the death of Hadrian, the Roman Pontiff, whom he had loved most of all his friends, he wept as much as if he had lost a brother, or a very dear son. He was by nature most ready to contract

---

follow this betrothal. Hruodrud had by Roderick, Count of Maine, a natural son, Lewis, who became Abbot of St. Denis, and died in 867.

[55] His eyes were put out by order of Lewis the Pious, and he died in consequence in 817.

friendships, and not only made friends easily, but clung to them persistently, and cherished most fondly those with whom he had
formed such ties. He was so careful of the
training of his sons and daughters that he
never took his meals without them when
he was at home, and never made a journey without them; his sons would ride
at his side, and his daughters follow him,
while a number of his body-guard, detailed
for their protection, brought up the rear.
Strange to say, although they were very
handsome women, and he loved them very
dearly, he was never willing to marry[44]
any of them to a man of their own nation
or to a foreigner, but kept them all at home
until his death, saying that he could not
dispense with their society. Hence, though
otherwise happy, he experienced the malig-
nity of fortune as far as they were concerned; yet he concealed his knowledge of the
rumours current in regard to them, and of

---

[44] He married Bertha to Angilbert. See Note 98

the suspicions entertained of their honour.[57]

XX. By óne of his concubines[58] he had a son, handsome in face, but hunchbacked, named Pepin, whom I omitted to mention in the list of his children. When Charles was at war with the Huns, and was wintering in Bavaria, this Pepin shammed sickness, and plotted against his father in company with some of the leading Franks, who seduced him with vain promises of the royal authority. When his deceit was discovered, and the conspirators

792

---

[57] See Note 54 and Note 98.

[58] According to Paulus Diaconus, "Gesta Epp. Mett." ("Mon. Germ. Script." ii. 265), and other authorities, the name of this concubine was Himiltrud. Pope Stephen II. (or III.) has been thought to refer to her as Charles's lawful wife, in a letter written by him in 770 to Charles and Carloman. Her son, Pepin, is named before Hildegard's sons in certain litanies compiled shortly after Charles's marriage with Fastrada. She is supposed by some to have been also the mother of Ruodhaid, mentioned in XVIII. Pepin the Hunchback died in 811.

were punished, his head was shaved, and he was suffered, in accordance with his wishes, to devote himself to a religious life in the monastery of Prüm. A formidable conspiracy against Charles had previously been set on foot in Ger- 785–786. many, but all the traitors were banished, some of them without mutilation, others after their eyes had been put out. Three of them only lost their lives; they drew their swords and resisted arrest, and, after killing several men, were cut down, because they could not be otherwise overpowered. It is supposed that the cruelty of Queen Fastrada was the primary cause of these plots, and they were both due to Charles's apparent acquiescence in his wife's cruel conduct, and deviation from the usual kindness and gentleness of his disposition. All the rest of his life he was regarded by every one with the utmost love and affection, so much so that not the least accusation of unjust rigour was ever made against him.

XXI. He liked foreigners, and was at great pains to take them under his protection. There were often so many of them, both in the palace and the kingdom, that they might reasonably have been considered a nuisance; but he, with his broad humanity, was very little disturbed by such annoyances, because he felt himself compensated for these great inconveniences by the praises of his generosity and the reward of high renown.

XXII. Charles was large and strong, and of lofty stature, though not disproportionately tall (his height is well known to have been seven times the length of his foot); the upper part of his head was round, his eyes very large and animated, nose a little long, hair fair, and face laughing and merry. Thus his appearance was always stately and dignified, whether he was standing or sitting; although his neck was thick and somewhat short, and his belly rather prominent; but the symmetry of the rest of his body concealed these defects.   His gait was

firm, his whole carriage manly, and his
voice clear, but not so strong as his size
led one to expect. His health was excellent, except during the four years preceding
his death, when he was subject to frequent
fevers; at the last he even limped a little
with one foot. Even in those years he con-
sulted rather his own inclinations than the
advice of physicians, who were almost hate-
ful to him, because they wanted him to give
up roasts, to which he was accustomed, and
to eat boiled meat instead. In accordance
with the national custom, he took frequent
exercise on horseback and in the chase, ac-
complishments in which scarcely any people in the world can equal the Franks. He
enjoyed the exhalations from natural warm
springs, and often practised swimming, in
which he was such an adept that none
could surpass him; and hence it was that
he built his palace at Aix-la-Chapelle, and
lived there constantly during his latter
years until his death. He used not only to
invite his sons to his bath, but his nobles

and friends, and now and then a troop of
his retinue or body-guard, so that a hundred or more persons sometimes bathed
with him.

XXIII. He used to wear the national,
that is to say, the Frank, dress—next his
skin a linen shirt and linen breeches, and
above these a tunic fringed with silk; while
hose fastened by bands covered his lower
limbs, and shoes his feet, and he protected
his shoulders and chest in winter by a close-
fitting coat of otter or marten skins.   Over
all he flung a blue cloak, and he always
had a sword girt about him, usually one
with a gold or silver hilt and belt; he sometimes carried a jewelled sword, but only on
great feast-days or at the reception of ambassadors from foreign nations.   He despised foreign costumes, however handsome,
and never allowed himself to be robed in
them, except twice in Rome, when he don-
ned the Roman tunic, chlamys, and shoes;
the first time at the request of Pope Ha-

drian,[59] the second to gratify Leo,[60] Hadrian's successor. On great feast-days he made use of embroidered clothes, and shoes bedecked with precious stones; his cloak was fastened by a golden buckle, and he appeared crowned with a diadem of gold and gems: but on other days his dress varied little from the common dress of the people.

XXIV. Charles was temperate in eating, and particularly so in drinking, for he abominated drunkenness in anybody, much more in himself and those of his household; but he could not easily abstain from food, and often complained that fasts injured his health. He very rarely gave entertainments, only on great feast-days, and then to large numbers of people. His meals ordinarily consisted of four courses, not counting the roast, which his huntsmen used to bring in on the spit; he was more fond of this than

[59] Hadrian I., 772-795.
[60] Leo III., 795-816.

of any other dish. While at table, he listen-
ed to reading or music. The subjects of
the readings were the stories and deeds of
olden time : he was fond, too, of St. Augus-
tine's books, and especially of the one en-
titled " The City of God." He was so mod-
erate in the use of wine and all sorts of
drink that he rarely allowed himself more
than three cups in the course of a meal.
In summer, after the midday meal, he would
eat some fruit, drain a single cup, put off
his clothes and shoes, just as he did for the
night, and rest for two or three hours. He
was in the habit of awaking and rising from
bed four or five times during the night.
While he was dressing and putting on his
shoes, he not only gave audience to his
friends, but if the Count of the Palace told
him of any suit in which his judgment was
necessary, he had the parties brought before him forthwith, took cognizance of the
case, and gave his decision, just as if he
were sitting on the judgment - seat. This
was not the only business that he transact-

ed at this time, but he performed any duty of the day whatever, whether he had to attend to the matter himself, or to give commands concerning it to his officers.

XXV. Charles had the gift of ready and fluent speech, and could express whatever he had to say with the utmost clearness. He was not satisfied with command of his native language merely, but gave attention to the study of foreign ones, and in particular was such a master of Latin that he could speak it as well as his native tongue; but he could understand Greek better than he could speak it. He was so eloquent, indeed, that he might have passed for a teacher of eloquence. He most zealously cultivated the liberal arts, held those who taught them in great esteem, and conferred great honours upon them. He took lessons in grammar of the deacon Peter of Pisa,[41]

------

[41] At the capture of Pavia in 774 (see VI., p. 24), Charles found Peter teaching there, and carried him off to instal him in his palace school. No work of his has reached us.

at that time an aged man. Another deacon, Albin of Britain, surnamed Alcuin,[43] a
man of Saxon extraction, who was the
greatest scholar of the day, was his teacher
in other branches of learning.   The King
spent much time and labour with him
studying rhetoric, dialectics, and especially astronomy; he learned to reckon, and
used to investigate the motions of the heav-
enly bodies most curiously, with an intelli-
gent scrutiny.   He also tried to write, and
used to keep tablets and blanks in bed
under his pillow, that at leisure hours he
might accustom his hand to form the letters; however, as he did not begin his ef-
forts in due season, but late in life, they
met with ill success.

XXVI. He cherished with the greatest
fervour and devotion the principles of the
Christian religion, which had been instilled
into him from infancy.   Hence it was that

---

[43] Alcuin was born at York in 735, came to
Charles's court about 782, and died Abbot of St.
Martin of Tours, in 804.

he built the beautiful basilica at Aix - la-
Chapelle, which he adorned with gold and
silver and lamps, and with rails and doors
of solid brass. He had the columns and
marbles for this structure brought from
Rome and Ravenna,[43] for he could not find
such as were suitable elsewhere. He was
a constant worshipper at this church as
long as his health permitted, going morning and evening, even after nightfall, besides attending mass; and he took care that
all the services there conducted should be
administered with the utmost possible pro-
priety, very often warning the sextons not
to let any improper or unclean thing be
brought into the building, or remain in it.
He provided it with a great number of
sacred vessels of gold and silver, and with
such a quantity of clerical robes that not
even the doorkeepers, who fill the humblest
office in the church, were obliged to wear
their every-day clothes when in the exer-

[43] See letter of Hadrian I. to Charles, in Jaffé's
"Monumenta Carolina," p. 268.

cise of their duties. He was at great pains.
to improve the church reading and psal-
mody, for he was well skilled in both, although he neither read in public nor sang,
except in a low tone and with others.

XXVII. He was very forward in succour-
ing the poor, and in that gratuitous generosity which the Greeks call alms, so much
so that he not only made a point of giving
in his own country and his own kingdom,
but when he discovered that there were
Christians living in poverty in Syria, Egypt,
and Africa, at Jerusalem, Alexandria, and
Carthage, he had compassion on their wants,
and used to send money over the seas to
them. The reason that he zealously strove
to make friends with the kings beyond seas
was that he might get help and relief to
the Christians living under their rule. He
cherished the Church of St. Peter the Apos-
tle at Rome above all other holy and sacred
places, and heaped its treasury with a vast
wealth of gold, silver, and precious stones.
He sent great and countless gifts to the

popes; and throughout his whole reign the wish that he had nearest at heart was to re-establish the ancient authority of the city of Rome under his care and by his influence, and to defend and protect the Church of St. Peter, and to beautify and enrich it out of his own store above all other churches. Although he held it in such veneration, he only repaired to Rome to pay his vows and make his supplications four times[44] during the whole forty-seven years[45] that he reigned.

XXVIII. When he made his last journey thither, he had also other ends in view. The Romans had inflicted **800.** many injuries upon the Pontiff Leo, tearing out his eyes and cutting out his tongue, so that he had been compelled to call upon the King for help. Charles accordingly went to Rome, to set in order the affairs of the Church, which were in great confusion, and passed the whole **Nov. 24.**

---

[44] In 774, 781, 787, and 800.
[45] See Note 30.

winter there.   It was then that he received
Dec. 25. the titles of Emperor and Augustus, to which he at first had such
an aversion that he declared that he would
not have set foot in the Church the day
that they were conferred, although it was a
great feast-day, if he could have foreseen
the design of the Pope.   He bore very patiently with the jealousy which the Roman
emperors showed upon his assuming these
titles, for they took this step very ill; and
by dint of frequent embassies and letters, in
which he addressed. them as brothers, he
made their haughtiness yield to his mag-
nanimity, a quality in which he was un-
questionably much their superior.

XXIX. It was after he had received the
imperial name that, finding the laws of his
people very defective (the Franks have two
sets of laws,[44] very different in many par-
ticulars), he determined to add what was
wanting, to reconcile the discrepancies, and

---

[44] The Salic and Ripuarian.

to correct what was vicious and wrongly cited in them. However, he went no further in this matter than to supplement the laws by a few capitularies, and those imperfect ones; but he caused the unwritten laws of all the tribes that came under his rule[67] to be compiled and reduced to writing. He also had the old rude songs that celebrate the deeds and wars of the ancient kings written out for transmission to posterity. He began a grammar of his native language. He gave the months names in his own tongue, in place of the Latin and barbarous names by which they were formerly known among the Franks. He likewise designated the winds by twelve appropriate names; there were hardly more than four distinctive ones in use before. He called January Wintarmanoth;[68] February, Hornung;[69] March, Lentzinmanoth;[70] April, Os-

---

[67] Of the Saxons, Frisians, and Thuringians.
[68] Winter month.
[69] Horn-shedding (of stags).
[70] Spring month.

tarmanoth ;[71] May, Winnemanoth ;[72] June,
Brachmanoth ;[73] July, Heuvimanoth ;[74] Au-
gust, Aranmanoth ;[75] September, Wituma-
noth ;[76] October, Windumemanoth ;[77] No-
vember, Herbistmanoth ;[78] December, Hei-
lagmanoth.[79] He styled the winds as follows : Subsolanus, Ostroniwint ; Eurus, Ost-
sundroni ; Euroauster, Sundostroni ; Auster,
Sundroni ; Austro - Africus, Sundwestroni ;
Africus, Westsundroni ; Zephyrus, Westroni ;
Caurus, Westnordroni ; Circius, Nordwestro-
ni ; Septentrio, Nordroni ; Aquilo, Nordos-
troni ; Vulturnus, Ostnordroni.[80]

---

[71] Easter month.
[72] Pasture month.
[73] Break (ground) month.
[74] Hay month.
[75] Ears (of grain) month.
[76] Wood month.
[77] Vintage month.
[78] Harvest month.
[79] Holy month.
[80] The compass, according to Charles, is box-
ed by twelve points therefore, as follows : N.,
N.E., E.N., E., E.S., S.E., S., S.W., W.S., W.,
W.N., N.W.

XXX. Towards the close of his life,
when he was broken by ill-health and old
age, he summoned Lewis, King of
Aquitania, his only surviving son   813.
by Hildegard, and gathered together all the
chief men of the whole kingdom of the
Franks in a solemn assembly. He appointed Lewis, with their unanimous consent,
to rule with himself over the whole kingdom, and constituted him heir to the imperial name; then, placing the diadem upon
his son's head, he bade him be proclaimed
Emperor and Augustus. This step was hail-
ed by all present with great favour, for it
really seemed as if God had prompted him
to it for the kingdom's good; it increased
the King's dignity, and struck no little ter-
ror into foreign nations. After sending his
son back to Aquitania, although weak from
age he set out to hunt, as usual, near his
palace at Aix-la-Chapelle, and passed the
rest of the autumn in the chase, returning
thither about the first of Novem-
ber. While wintering there, he   Nov. 1

was seized, in the month of January, with
a high fever, and took to his bed.
As soon as he was taken sick, he
prescribed for himself abstinence from food,
as he always used to do in case of fever,
thinking that the disease could be driven
off, or at least mitigated, by fasting. Besides the fever, he suffered from a pain in
the side, which the Greeks call pleurisy;
but he still persisted in fasting, and in keeping up his strength only by draughts taken
at very long intervals.   He died January
twenty - eighth, the seventh day
from the time that he took to his
bed, at nine o'clock in the morning, after
partaking of the holy communion, in the
72d year of his age[81] and the 47th of his
reign.

XXXI. His body was washed and cared
for in the usual manner, and was then car-

[81] Admitting the date of Charles's birth to have
been April 2d, 742 (see Note 12), he was not quite
seventy years and ten months old when he
died.

ried to the church, and interred amid the greatest lamentations of all the people. There was some question at first where to lay him, because in his lifetime he had given no directions as to his burial; but at length all agreed that he could nowhere be more honourably entombed than in the very basilica that he had built in the town at his own expense, for love of God and our Lord Jesus Christ, and in honour of the Holy and Eternal Virgin, His Mother. He was buried there the same day that he died, and a gilded arch was erected above his tomb with his image and an inscription. The words of the inscription were as follows: "In this tomb lies the body of Charles, the Great and Orthodox Emperor, who gloriously extended the kingdom of the Franks, and reigned prosperously for forty-seven years."[32] He died at the age of seventy, in the year of our Lord 814, the 7th Indiction, on the 28th day of January."

---

[32] See Note 30.

XXXII. Very many omens had portend-
ed his approaching end, a fact that he had
recognized as well as others.   Eclipses both
of the sun and moon were very frequent
during the last three years of his life, and
a black spot was visible on the sun for the
space of seven days.   The gallery between
the basilica and the palace, which he had
built at great pains and labour, fell in sudden ruin to the ground on the day of the
Ascension of our Lord.   The wooden bridge
over the Rhine at Mayence, which he had
caused to be constructed with admirable
skill, at the cost of ten years' hard work, so
that it seemed as if it might last forever, was
813.   so completely consumed in three
May.   hours by an accidental fire that
not a single splinter of it was left, except
what was under water.   Moreover, one day
           in his last campaign into Saxony
810.   against Godfred, King of the Danes,
Charles himself saw a ball of fire fall sud-
denly from the heavens with a great light,
just as he was leaving camp before sunrise

to set out on the march. It rushed across
the clear sky from right to left, and every-
body was wondering what was the mean-
ing of the sign, when the horse which he
was riding gave a sudden plunge, head
foremost, and fell, and threw him to the
ground so heavily that his cloak-buckle
was broken and his sword-belt shattered;
and after his servants had hastened to him
and relieved him of his arms, he could
not rise without their assistance. He hap-
pened to have a javelin in his hand when
he was thrown, and this was struck from
his grasp with such force that it was found
lying at a distance of twenty feet or more
from the spot. Again, the palace at Aix-
la-Chapelle frequently trembled, the roofs
of whatever buildings he tarried in kept
up a continual crackling noise, the basilica
in which he was afterwards buried was
struck by lightning, and the gilded ball
that adorned the pinnacle of the roof was
shattered by the thunder-bolt and hurled
upon the bishop's house adjoining. In this

same basilica, on the margin of the cornice
that ran around the interior, between the
upper and lower tiers of arches, a legend
was inscribed in red letters, stating who
was the builder of the temple, the last
words of which were *Karolus Princeps*.
The year that he died it was remarked by
some, a few months before his decease, that
the letters of the word *Princeps* were so ef-
faced as to be no longer decipherable. But
Charles despised, or affected to despise, all
these omens, as having no reference whatever to him.

XXXIII. It had been his intention to
make a will, that he might give some share
in the inheritance to his daughters and the
children of his concubines; but it was begun too late and could not be finished.
Three years before his death, however, he
made a division of his treasures, money,
clothes, and other movable goods
811   in the presence of his friends and
servants, and called them to witness it,
that their voices might insure the ratifi-

cation of the disposition thus made. He
had a summary drawn up of his wishes
regarding this distribution of his property, the terms and text of which are as
follows :

"In the name of the Lord God, the Al-
mighty Father, Son, and Holy Ghost. This
is the inventory and division dictated by
the most glorious and most pious Lord
Charles, Emperor Augustus, in the 811th
year of the Incarnation of our Lord Jesus
Christ, in the 43d year of his reign in
France and 37th in Italy, the 11th of his
empire, and the 4th Indiction, which con-
siderations of piety and prudence have
determined him, and the favour of God
enabled him, to make of his treasures and
money ascertained this day to be in his
treasure-chamber. In this division he is
especially desirous to provide not only that
the largess of alms which Christians usually
make of their possessions shall be made for
himself in due course and order out of his

wealth, but also that his heirs shall be free
from all doubt, and know clearly what be-
longs to them, and be able to share their
property by suitable partition without liti-
gation or strife. With this intention and
to this end he has first divided all his sub-
stance and movable goods ascertained to
be in his treasure-chamber on the day aforesaid in gold, silver, precious stones, and
royal ornaments into three lots, and has
subdivided and set off two of the said lots
into twenty-one parts, keeping the third entire. The first two lots have been thus subdivided into twenty-one parts because there
are in his kingdom twenty-one[88] recognized
metropolitan cities, and in order that each
archbishopric may receive by way of alms,
at the hands of his heirs and friends, one
of the said parts, and that the archbishop
who shall then administer its affairs shall
take the part given to it, and share the same
with his suffragans in such manner that one

[88] There were, in fact, twenty-two. Narbonne
is omitted from the list for reasons unknown.

third shall go to the Church, and the remaining two thirds be divided among the suffragans. The twenty-one parts into which the first two lots are to be distributed, according to the number of recognized metropolitan cities, have been set apart one from another, and each has been put aside by itself in a box labelled with the name of the city for which it is destined. The names of the cities to which this alms or largess is to be sent are as follows: Rome, Ravenna, Milan, Friuli, Grado, Cologne, Mayence, Salzburg, Treves, Sens, Besançon, Lyons, Rouen, Rheims, Arles, Vienne, Moutiers-en-Tarantaise, Embrun, Bordeaux, Tours, and Bourges. The third lot, which he wishes to be kept entire, is to be bestowed as follows: While the first two lots are to be divided into the parts aforesaid, and set aside under seal, the third lot shall be employed for the owner's daily needs, as property which he shall be under no obligation to part with in order to the fulfilment of any vow, and this as long as he shall be in

the flesh,. or consider it necessary for his
use. But upon his death, or voluntary renunciation of the affairs of this world, this
said lot shall be divided into four parts,
and one thereof shall be added to the aforesaid twenty-one parts; the second shall be
assigned to his sons and daughters, and to
the sons and daughters of his sons, to be
distributed among them in just and equal
partition ; the third, in accordance with the
custom common among Christians, shall be
devoted to the poor; and the fourth shall
go to the support of the men-servants and
maid-servants on duty in the palace. It is
his wish that to this said third lot of the
whole amount, which consists, as well as
the rest, of gold and silver, shall be added
all the vessels and utensils of brass, iron,
and other metals, together with the arms,
clothing, and other movable goods, costly
and cheap, adapted to divers uses, as hang-
ings. coverlets, carpets, woollen stuffs, leath-
ern articles, pack-saddles, and whatsoever
shall be found in his treasure-chamber and

wardrobe at that time, in order that thus the parts of the said lot may be augmented, and the alms distributed reach more persons. He ordains that his chapel—that is to say, its church property, as well that which he has provided and collected as that which came to him by inheritance from his father—shall remain entire, and not be dissevered by any partition whatever. If, however, any vessels, books, or other articles be found therein which are certainly known not to have been given by him to the said chapel, whoever wants them shall have them on paying their value at a fair estimation. He likewise commands that the books which he has collected in his library in great numbers shall be sold for fair prices to such as want them, and the money received therefrom given to the poor. It is well known that among his other property and treasures are three silver tables, and one very large and massive golden one. He directs and commands that the square silver table, upon which there is a represen-

tation of the city of Constantinople, shall
be sent to the Basilica of St. Peter the Apos-
tle at Rome, with the other gifts destined
therefor; that the round one, adorned with
a delineation of the city of Rome, shall be
given to the Episcopal Church at Ravenna;
that the third, which far surpasses the other
two in weight and in beauty of workman-
ship, and is made in three circles, showing
the plan of the whole universe,[84] drawn with
skill and delicacy, shall go, together with
the golden table, fourthly above mentioned,
to increase that lot which is to be devoted
to his heirs and to alms.

This deed, and the dispositions thereof, he
has made and appointed in the presence of
the bishops, abbots, and counts able to be
present, whose names are hereto subscribed:

---

[84] The Ptolemaic universe, as modified by Aris-
totle and Hipparchus. The Primum Mobile was
added later. For a diagram and brief descrip-
tion of the Ptolemaic universe, see Masson's
Introduction to "Paradise Lost" in his edition
of Milton's "Poetical Works."

Bishops—Hildebald,[85] Ricolf,[86] Arno,[87] Wol-
far,[88] Bernoin,[89] Laidrad,[90] John,[91] Theo-
dulf,[92] Jesse,[93] Heito,[94] Waltgaud.[95] Abbots
—Fredugis,[96] Adalung,[97] Angilbert,[98] Ir-

---

[85] Cologne.
[86] Mayence.
[87] Salzburg.
[88] Rheims.
[89] Besançon.
[90] Lyons.
[91] Arles.
[92] Orleans.
[93] Amiens.
[94] Basle.
[95] Liege.
[96] St. Bertin in St. Omer. (St. Martin of Tours
—Jaffé.)
[97] St. Vedast in Arras. (Lorsch.—Jaffé.)
[98] Angilbert had been First Dean of the Chap-
ter in the palace of Pepin, King of Italy, Duke of
Maritime France, and Charles's Prime-minister;
but in 790 he retired to the Monastery of Centu-
lum in St. Riquier, and became its abbot several
years previous to his death, in 814. He was bred
at court, and had an intrigue with Charles's
daughter Bertha, who had two sons by him—
Hartnidus and Nithardus the historian. Charles
legitimated this union in 787. Bertha took the
veil when Angilbert became a monk. Little ex-

E   6

mino." Counts—Walacho,[100] Meginher, Otulf, Stephen, Unruoch, Burchard, Meginhard, Hatto, Rihwin, Edo, Ercangar, Gerold, Bero, Hildiger, Rocculf."

Charles's son Lewis, who by the grace of God succeeded him, after examining this summary, took pains to fulfil all its conditions most religiously as soon as possible after his father's death.

814.

---

cept the "Carmen de Karolo Magno" remains to show Angilbert's literary ability.

[99] St. Germain in Paris.

[100] He was afterwards Abbot of Corvey.

GENEALOGICAL TABLE.

THE FAMILY OF CHARLES AND HILDEGARD.

Pepin of Heristal ;
d. 714.

Charles Martel ;
d. 741.

Pepin the Short ; m Berthrada ;
d. 768.

Gisela ; Rodthaid, Adelaide, Carloman ;
d. 783.

Parentage uncertain.

Gerold ;
d. 799.

Hildegard ;
d. 783.

m. 772 ;

Charles ;
b. 742 ;
d. 814.

Gisela ;
d. 810.

Charles ;
b. 772 ;
d. 4 Dec.,
811.

Adelaide ;
b. 774 ;
d. young.

Hruodrud ;
b. 775 ;
d. 6 June,
810.

Bertha ;
b. about 775.

Carloman ;
or
Pepin ;
b. 776 ;
d. 8 July,
810.

Lewis ;
b. 778 ;
d. 840.

Twins.

Lothar ;
b. 778 ;
d. 780.

Gisela ;
b. 781.

Hildegard ;
b. 782 ;
d. 783.

www.ingramcontent.com/pod-product-compliance
Lightning Source LLC
Chambersburg PA
CBHW030002030726
47499CB00008B/2855